For Frankie
Emma Garcia

First American edition published in 2007
by Boxer Books Limited.

Distributed in the United States and Canada
by Sterling Publishing Co., Inc.
387 Park Avenue South, New York, NY 10016-8810

First published in Great Britain in 2007
by Boxer Books Limited.
www.boxerbooks.com

Original idea, text and illustrations copyright © 2007 Emma Garcia

ISBN 13: 978-1-905417-58-2
ISBN 10: 1-905417-58-6

3 5 7 9 10 8 6 4 2

Printed in China

Tip Tip Dig Dig

Emma Garcia

Boxer Books

Look at all this mess!
What can we do
with it?

With the digger
we can

Dig

Dig

Dig

With the mixer we can

With the crane
we can

With the
dump truck
we can

Tip
Tip Tip
Tip

With the bulldozer we can

Push
Push
Push

With the
road roller
we can

So the digger digs a hole

and the mixer
mixes the asphalt.

The dump truck tips the sand

and the crane lifts
the wood.

The bulldozer
pushes the soil

and the road roller
rolls a path.

What did we do with all that mess?

We dug.

We mixed.

We lifted.

We
tipped.

We
pushed.

We rolled
and we...

...made an adventure

playground!